This Little Tiger book belongs to:

Mrs Davies

For Mortimer

LITTLE TIGER PRESS

An imprint of Magi Publications

1 The Coda Centre, 189 Munster Road, London SW6 6AW

www.littletigerpress.com

First published in Great Britain 2001

This edition published 2005

Text and illustrations copyright © Ruth Galloway 2001

Ruth Galloway has asserted her right to be identified

as the author and illustrator of this work under the

Copyright, Designs and Patents Act, 1988.

All rights reserved • ISBN-13: 978-1-84506-241-5

ISBN-10: 1-84506-241-8

Printed in China

5 7 9 10 8 6

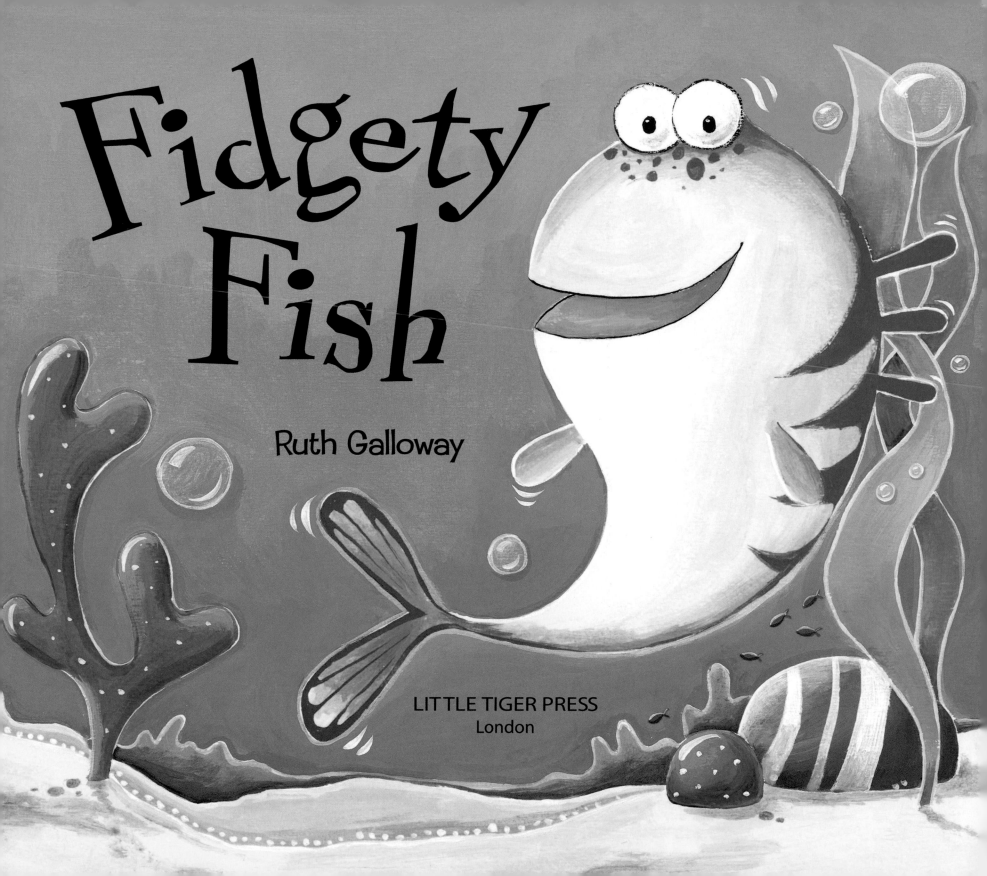

Fidgety
Fish

Ruth Galloway

LITTLE TIGER PRESS

London

Tiddler was always fidgeting.

He wriggled and squiggled,

he darted and giggled . . .

until his mum got fed up with him.
"Go out into the sea and swim
till you're tired, but watch out for
the Big Fish," she said.
So Tiddler swam out of his cave.

He dived and he flipped,

he leapt and he dipped.

He sped faster than a rocket . . . .

and glided gently like a swan,
letting the sea currents fan his fins.

But he still didn't feel tired!

There were limpets that clung,

and jellyfish that stung.

Tiddler swam on towards
the big, red starfish . . .

and butted it gently with his nose.
The starfish just smiled, so . . .

Tiddler asked the clickety-clackety crab to play, but it scuttled off into the seaweed.

Tiddler came to a big, dark cave.
It looked much more exciting
than his cave back home,
and Tiddler swam in . . .

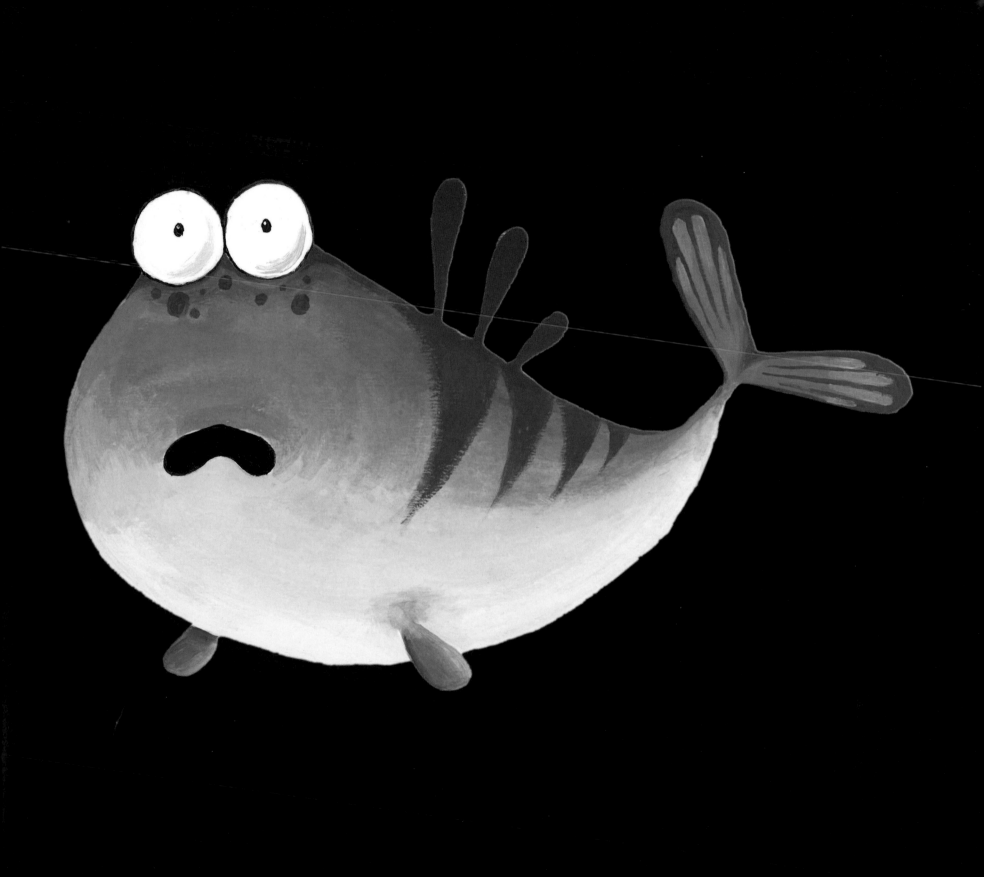

Tiddler was trapped inside the Big Fish!

He trembled
and shivered,

and he shook and
he quivered . . .

until the Big Fish's tummy began to feel very
funny indeed.

It rumbled and grumbled,
it turned and it tumbled.
It fluttered and groaned,
and mumbled and moaned.

Suddenly the Big Fish
did an enormous . . .

out shot Tiddler . . .

past the jellyfish,

and the clickety-clackety
crab hiding in the weeds,

past the starfish . . .

and straight through his own front door!

"I hope you've used up all that energy," said his mum . . .

but she would have to wait
until the morning to hear
about his adventures,
because Tiddler
was already
fast asleep!

Dive into the world of
Little Tiger Press

QUIET!

Paul Bright
illustrated by
Guy Parker-Rees

The Crunching Munching Caterpillar

Sheridan Cain
Jack Tickle

The Very Noisy Night

Diana Hendry
illustrated by Jane Chapman

The Very Lazy Ladybird

Isobel Finn & Jack Tickle

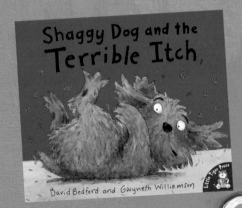

Shaggy Dog and the Terrible Itch

David Bedford and Gwyneth Williamson

For information regarding any of the above titles
or for our catalogue, please contact us:

Little Tiger Press, 1 The Coda Centre,
189 Munster Road, London SW6 6AW, UK
Tel: 020 7385 6333 Fax: 020 7385 7333
E-mail: info@littletiger.co.uk
www.littletigerpress.com